# Spoon Boy

*Written by Jim Cruise*

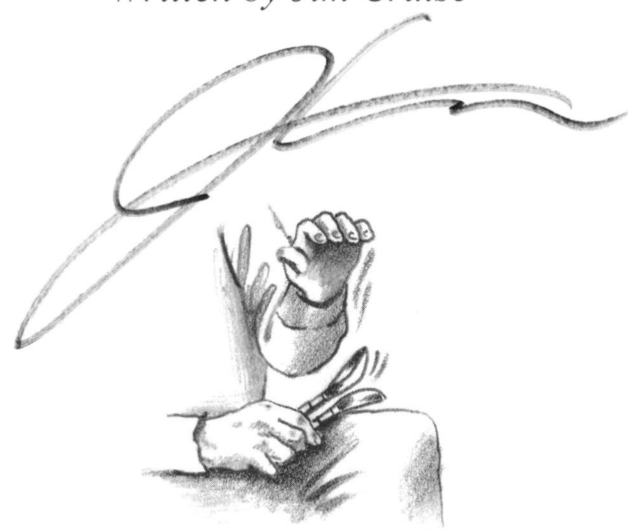

*Cover illustration by Marianna Heule*

*Interior illustrations by Jon Post*

ISBN: 978-0-9667757-1-6



Published by Faustina Publishing
318 White Tail Court
Grandville, MI 49418

Printed in the U.S.A.

Sixth printing, May 2012

*For Jean, Valerie, Kevin, Natalie, Bridget and Isabelle.*
*My wife and children for having to put up with a Spoon Man*
*as a Husband and Dad.*

*Acknowledgements*

So many people have asked me for nearly 30 years
how I got started playing the spoons, and how I possibly
support a wife, 5 children and pay a mortgage.
The simple answer,  it's only by God's mercy and grace.

# Contents

Chapter 1

# The Music

*Thud, thud, rattle, rattle, boom, boom* went my bedroom walls as the music seeped in. It was the early 1970s and disco music was king. *Squeak! Creak*! My old bed was making noises as I tossed and turned trying to get to sleep. Every time I moved, it squeaked. I rolled over—*squeak!* I got out of bed—*squeak!* I got into bed—*squeak!* It was as if I could not move an inch without making noise.

I did not have to worry about being heard because the music was shaking the walls. How long would my mother continue to play her disco music? It was cleaning night and she was working to the beat. She wore her favorite flannel nightgown—yellow with hot air balloons. It hung just above her ankles. She would glide through the house with a Hoover vacuum in her hand dancing to her favorite records.

It was a sticky, humid evening in early May, and I was required to go to bed at 8 p.m. because it was a school night. My Dad was working the night shift at General Motors. He was not home much because he was working so hard to provide for our family.

My wooden closet doors always stayed closed. Open closets scared me, while I was trying to fall asleep. If I got scared, I could hide under my bed. There was plenty of room to hide, if you could put up with all the dust underneath! My floor was wooden, so it creaked even louder than my bed.

"What time is it?" whispered Susie, my sister, who was one year younger than I was. She had black scraggly hair. Because we were so close in age, we did not always get along. She was eight years old and in the third grade. I was nine years old and in the fourth grade. I ignored my sister's question because I did not feel like playing the time and day game.

"What time is it?" she shouted louder.

Her bedroom was right across the hall from mine. Susie had to share her bedroom with our little sister Lori, who was three years old. She was still bald with just a little bit of red fuzz on her head. We all called her "tornado baby." Wherever she went, she made a mess. My sister Lori did not have to go to bed now because she did not have to go to school. Susie and I hated that.

I gave in and shouted back. "What day is it today?"

"Tuesday," she answered.

"No, it's not. It's Friday," I said.

"It's Sunday," she said.

"You're wrong; it's Wednesday," I insisted. "What time is it now?" I asked.

"It's midnight," she said.

"No, it's not. It's nine," I stated.

"No, it's eight," said Susie.

My sister and I could not agree about anything except that Lori was spoiled and we were both jealous.

Suddenly, the music stopped.

"Jimmy, is that you?" my mother screamed down the hallway.

"No," I shouted. "It's Susie."

"He's lying, Mom," she whined.

"Both of you get back to bed and be quiet," my mother yelled again.

*BA, BA, bum, pa, dada.* My mother turned the music

on more quietly this time and went back to cleaning. I especially liked the different rhythms. I imagined I was playing drums with the band.

"I like the rhythms and I like the beats and I'm not ready to fall asleep," I whispered across the hall to Susie. She agreed with me about not sleeping. It was a perfect night for spying.

Chapter 2

# The Spies

Susie and I met in the hallway. We made sure to move only when the songs were playing and never in between songs. No one could see us or hear us as we hurried down the narrow hallway into the bathroom. We made it to the bathroom without being caught.

The bathroom was painted burnt orange and had one window facing our family room. The angles of the windows in both rooms made us able to peer into the family room. The music was still playing and the vacuum still running. This made us feel safe.

Nothing was more fun than spying, unless of course, we were discovered, and my heart was chugging like a train, knowing that we could be caught. There she sat, the spoiled, red, fuzzy "tornado baby," legally named Lori.

"What's that smell?" my sister Susie asked.

"It's popcorn," I stated. "Look, she's watching TV with a big bowl of popcorn."

"That's not fair. We have to go to bed at eight. She can stay up and have snacks!" I said to Susie.

"Wait!" exclaimed Susie. "She's eating something else."

"It looks like a bowl of our ice cream, the flavor we picked out when we went shopping with Dad," I said.

"You mean our strawberry swirl ice cream?" she asked.

"Yes," I said with my eyes narrowing into a glare.

Then Susie made a colossal mistake. For some reason, she decided to turn on the bathroom light. When Lori saw the bathroom light go on, she started to scream. "Look, look, Mommy," she said accusingly, pointing at our surprised faces that were peering back through the bathroom window. My mother shut off the vacuum and the music.

"Why did you turn on the light?" I yelled at Susie.

"I dropped my favorite penny on the floor," she said in a panicked voice. Susie had a shiny penny that she clutched wherever she went.

"Shut off the light. We've got to get out of here!" I whispered cautiously.

Lori kept shouting, "Look, Jimmy and Susie are in the bathroom!"

*Click* went the light switch. We tiptoed again through the hallway into our bedrooms and back into bed. *Creak! Squeak!*

"Oh no," I said. I had forgotten to climb into it gently.

"Jimmy!" screamed my mother. "What are you doing out of bed?"

My tornado baby sister Lori walked with my mother to our bedrooms for the questioning.

"I was thirsty," I blurted out.

"I suppose Susie was thirsty also?" she asked.

"I saw her, too, Mommy," said Lori.

I could see Lori now giggling jubilantly with a ring of strawberry swirl ice cream around her mouth.

"You're both in bed early tomorrow evening. You know the rules," she said. "You have a drink of water before you go to bed, not after."

"Yes, Mother," we both said together.

"Mom, what was that music you were playing?" I asked trying to change the subject.

“It was the Bee Gees,” she said.

“Mom, I wish I could play the drums with that band. If only I had a drum set,” I said with my puppy dog eyes.

“Maybe Grandpa could show you a cool trick with spoons,” she said.

“What do you mean?” I asked.

“Goodnight, Jimmy, we’ll talk about it some other time.”

Then I heard the music again. This time, the songs were a little quieter.

I whispered sleepily to my sister Susie, “What day is it?” She gave no response. I figured she was asleep and the fun was over, so I closed my eyes and tried to fall asleep.

*“What do my grandpa’s spoons have to do with playing the drums?”* I wondered.

I gave a big yawn and started to dream about becoming a rock-n-roll drummer.

Chapter 3

# Mr. Phillips

"Knock it off!" said Mr. Phillips, my fourth grade teacher. I was drumming on my desk to the Bee Gees. Mr. Phillips was a new teacher at our school Meadowlawn Elementary. He always wore a white button-down short-sleeved shirt. His arms were as hairy as a gorilla, and he always seemed to be wet underneath his armpits. The sweat marks under his arms looked like the state of Texas.

Mr. Phillips had the coolest pencil trick. "See this pencil," he said. "I can make it look like rubber." He grabbed the yellow #2 pencil by its tip and shook it vigorously up and down. It looked like a limp noodle. I could not believe it. When he stopped shaking it, the pencil was back to normal. Mr. Phillips had many cool things he did in the classroom compared to the other teachers.

I understood well what his classroom rules were. I was a kid in constant motion. I think Mr. Phillips was stuck with me because he knew how to handle my tendency to disrupt the classroom. I do not think the other fourth grade teachers could have controlled me.

"Jimmy, this is your last warning," Mr. Phillips said sternly, looking into my eyes.

I just could not help it. I loved the rhythms and the beat of the music. My mom's favorite songs were echoing in my brain and I just had to drum to them. This drumming did not impress Mr. Phillips at all. I thought I was quite impressive.

"Jimmy, that's it," Mr. Phillips said angrily.

"I'm sorry, I'm sorry, I'll stop now," I said apologetically.

"Sorry is not good enough this time. You've ignored my warnings twice. Up to the chalk board, now," he commanded.

Even though Mr. Phillips disciplined me, I still liked him a lot as a teacher because he was young and fun. The classroom was all in a buzz because I was in trouble again. Mr. Phillips took a piece of chalk and drew a small circle on the dark green chalkboard. Because I had gotten in so much trouble throughout the school year, I knew the purpose of the circle. I was required to put my nose in the middle of the circle. The problem was that the circle was made just high enough that I had to stand on my tiptoes to place my nose in it. After a while, it was painful for my legs and back. There is nothing like smelling chalk dust powder in the early morning. Although I was pressed up against the chalkboard, I still was able to hum a song, quietly drumming my fingers secretly. Over time, I think the chalkboard became indented from my face. In fact, if the sun shone in the classroom at the right angle, you could see the outline of my nose.

Occasionally, Mr. Phillips would bring in his guitar and play some songs. This made me want to drum even more. One time I asked him if I could join along. He said no because he did not want me to take over the classroom with my display of desktop rhythms.

Mr. Phillips announced that we were having a talent show for the first time at Meadowlawn Elementary. Tryouts were taking place after school on Wednesday. I had a few days to figure out what I would do. I could not recall anyone telling me I had any type of special talent, except for getting into trouble.

Grandma and Grandpa were coming over that evening for dinner. Maybe Grandpa could show me that spoon trick about which my mom was talking.

Chapter 4

# Grandma and Grandpa

As I approached the front of our house, I smelled something horrible. The pungent odor grew worse as I stepped through the doorway.

"Jimmy, hurry; get inside and wash your hands. Your Irish grandpa and grandma are coming over for dinner," said my mother.

"I know, Mom. I can tell by the smell," I said, while the nausea built up in my gut.

It was stinking boiled cabbage soup. "Yuck," I said quietly so my mother could not hear me. It smelled like one of Lori's dirty diapers.

My grandpa was tall and somewhat thin. His hair was all white. My grandma wore funny-looking cat eyeglasses. She was bringing her world famous potato salad this evening. It was my dad's favorite. I never tried her potato salad because I do not like cold, lumpy white stuff. My dad was gone this evening working the night shift again.

I was so excited about my grandma and grandpa coming that I decided to meet them at the street corner. I jumped on my green metallic bike with the yellow banana seat and peddled as fast as I could up to the corner, about a block away. I was so excited when company came over; I could hardly wait to greet them.

Off in the distance, I looked at the oncoming traffic. I was never allowed to cross this busy street, so I always stopped at the corner. I was searching for a plum-colored, four-door Oldsmobile that had a little bit of rust on the front of the hood.

"There it is," I said aloud to myself.

I started to wave my arms vigorously. Grandpa started to honk when he saw me, and I peddled my bike alongside them.

Grandma shouted out the car window, "Jimmy, you be careful. Don't get so close to our car."

"Come on Grandpa, I'll race you to the house," I shouted back, ignoring Grandma's warning.

I peddled faster and faster.

"How fast am I going, Grandpa?" I said, breathing heavily.

"You're going about twenty miles per hour," said Grandpa.

When we all arrived at my house, I quickly got off my bike and kissed Grandma and Grandpa hello.

"Jimmy, you're always so excited about everything," Grandma said.

"Grandpa," I said impatiently. "We're having a talent show at our school this Friday and I need some ideas."

"Sure." Grandpa said, scratching his white head.

"My mom said you could do something cool with spoons. Show me now. Grandpa, now," I demanded.

"Sure, I'll show you. It'll cost you ten dollars," said Grandpa chuckling.

"What?" I exclaimed.

"Just joking, Jimmy," said Grandpa. He sniffed the air and smiled. "I know that delicious smell! Your mom made us cabbage soup, didn't she?"

With a frown on my face, I said, "Yes."

My dad had told me that Grandpa could not smell because he smoked too many cigarettes. My dad figured toxic chemicals in the smoke permanently damaged Grandpa's sense of smell. I guess my dad had been wrong, or maybe the soup was so powerfully smelly, nothing could stop the odor.

"Let's go in to eat. Your grandma brought her famous potato salad. Are you hungry?" he said.

"Not really," I said, thinking how I could make it look like I was eating by swirling the soup around in my bowl.

After my sisters and I choked down the soup, it was time to talk to Grandpa.

Chapter 5

# How to Play the Spoons

"Jimmy, I'm going to show you how to play the spoons. Watch this," he said.

My grandpa began to slap the spoons from one leg to another. Then he dragged the spoons down his extended fingers, making a rolling sound.

"Wow! That is so cool. It sounded like you were playing drums," I said. "Can you show me how to do that for the talent show?"

"Let's take it one step at a time," he said. "The first thing we have to do is find a pair of matching spoons."

I opened the silverware drawer in the kitchen. The spoons were gleaming like a bunch of silver coins in a pirate's chest.

"Aha, here's a perfect pair," I said excitedly.

I handed the spoons over to my grandpa's purple-stained hands. My grandpa worked at a printing press his whole life. He always had color traces of light blues and purples under his fingernails and fingers. One time while working on the printing press, my grandpa was cutting papers and did not get his left index finger out quickly enough. Half of Grandpa's finger was cut off. Although he was missing part of his finger, he could still play the spoons incredibly.

"Let's go to the porch, Grandpa, where we can find some peace and quiet," I said.

"Now with the matching pair of spoons, you put them back to back. Grab the spoons like you were going to shake someone's hand. Now, you put your pointer finger between the spoon handles. Make a fist with the remaining fingers around the spoons," he said.

"You just need one finger?" I asked.

"All you need is your pointer finger," said Grandpa. "See the space in between the two backs of the spoons? That's how you get the clicking sound. When the backs of the spoons hit together, you get a click. Without a space, you'll never get any click."

"No space, no click. No space, no click," I repeated.

"When you hit the two spoons together, tap down lightly on your leg. Then place the palm of your hand over the spoons and tap upward lightly onto your palm. When you tap down, you get a click, and when you tap up, you get a click. You want to move just your wrist up and down and not your whole arm," he said.

My Grandpa showed off his talents once more by playing the spoons off his legs, arms, chest, chin, and feet.

"Wow!" I said amazed. "Who needs a drum set when you can play spoons like that?"

"Now you try it, Jimmy," said Grandpa.

As soon as I tried, they immediately fell apart in my hands.

"I just can't do it like you, Grandpa," I said discouraged. I was ready to quit after trying just one time. My grandpa could tell I was frustrated.

"Let me tell you a little secret, Jimmy. I learned this while watching the soldiers around me in World War II. Do you know what kind of soldiers our captain liked the most? They were the soldiers who were afraid, who were knocked down, who wanted to give up, but they didn't.

They kept picking themselves up and moving forward through the battles. Pick up those spoons and try it again," Grandpa commanded.

I was surprised to learn my grandpa was in the war.

"We'd better get going," yelled Grandma out the window to Grandpa.

"Thanks for the delicious soup," they both said to my mother.

"Thanks for the spoon-playing lesson, Grandpa," I shouted.

"Spoon-playing lesson?" my mother said. "Time to hide our spoons."

I immediately went to my bedroom and tried to play the spoons. My grandpa made it look so easy, but they kept coming apart in my hand. This was going to take some practice. No matter how I held the spoons, they kept falling apart.

"I'm not going to give up. I'm going to fight through it. The talent show is coming up in a week," I thought.

That evening, I discovered another problem. Not

only was it difficult to hold the spoons, I now had bruises up and down my leg. It was not a good idea to play spoons in shorts. My legs were starting to turn a deep purple color like my grandpa's hands. They were swelling up so badly they looked like they belonged on an elephant. I could hardly move.

"Time for bed," Mom shouted to us.

"What day is it today?" whispered my irritating sister Susie.

She tried to start our evening ritual.

"I'm too tired and sore to play that game tonight," I said while clutching my spoons and legs.

"What time is it?" Susie said.

I just rolled over, ignored her, said my prayers, and dreamed about becoming a spoon-playing star.

Chapter 6

# The Talent Show

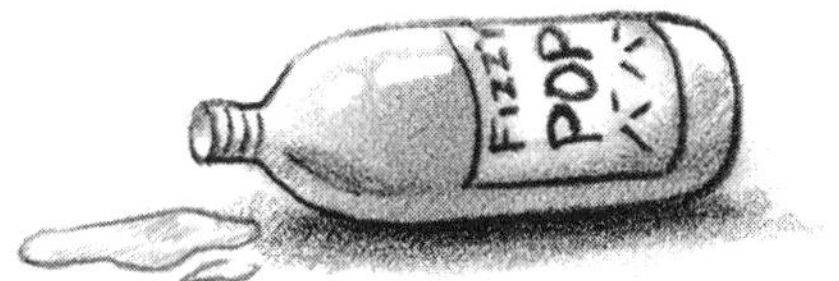

"School's out. Let's go," I shouted in the classroom. Mr. Phillips just glared at me.

The tryouts were taking place after school in the gymnasium. Mrs. Wescott and Mrs. Brown were the teachers in charge. My sister Susie had no interest in what she called the "dumb" talent show. The only thing Susie was good at was making fingernail marks in my skin when she got angry with me.

The girls seemed to either sing or dance. Valerie, a petite girl with short blonde hair and red wire-rimmed glasses, was the best singer in the fourth grade—maybe even in the whole school. Too Tall Stephanie, the tallest girl in the fifth grade, was the best dancer. She was taller than some teachers were. About twenty girls tried out in total.

Now, it was the boys' turn. From kindergarten to fifth grade, the boys tried out. Mrs. Wescott and Mrs. Brown were not impressed with any of the boys.

Burping Bobby belched out The Star-Spangled Banner. He had to stop halfway through because of nausea from drinking a two-liter soda. It was the only way he could get enough gas in his stomach to burp. Kevin was also in the fifth grade. He whistled Beethoven's Fifth Symphony. About two minutes into his routine, he passed out from hyperventilation, which happens when you do not take in enough oxygen. My friend P. J. told jokes that were not funny, but he did do a cool magic trick.

Now, it was my turn. My heart was beating as fast as a runaway train. I was so nervous that I did not notice the huge sticky spot on the gym floor. The janitor must have missed mopping this spot after lunch. My basketball shoes stuck to the floor, and I could not take a step. I removed my shoes and tried walking in my white socks up to the stage. This was not a good idea either. To my embarrassment, my socks stuck right to the floor a few inches from my shoes. Now, I was barefoot. The teachers and students started to laugh. They thought I was doing a comedy act. Fortunately, the janitor came by and put some water on the floor, mopping up the gigantic sticky mess. He then handed me my socks and shoes before they got wet. I was now ready to audition.

The music I chose was "Rockin' Robin" by the Jackson 5. The palms of my hands were dripping with sweat like a leaky faucet. The music started, and I tried to remember what my grandpa had taught me. The spoons kept falling apart in my hands. The students started to laugh. Again, they thought I was doing a comedy act. The teachers tried to quiet the students as I finished my two-minute routine. It was a disaster. I had not spent enough time practicing, and it showed. I slowly walked off the stage with my head hung low.

"Good try, Jimmy," said Bobby as he burped.

Bobby was just trying to be kind.

"Thanks," I said back. "You did a nice job, too."

Now it was just a matter of waiting for the results. I tossed and turned all night long wondering if I would be chosen.

Chapter 7

# The Strike

The next morning, tensions were very high. The teachers posted the results of the tryouts on the old discolored red bulletin board hanging outside the school's office. The teachers were unimpressed with the entire group of boys. None of the boys made the show!

"What's the problem?" asked Johnny.

"I can't believe it," Burping Bobby yelled. "I would like to see one of those teachers do what I did."

All the third, fourth, and fifth grade boys were in an uproar.

Someone screamed, "We're not going to take this."

The girls did not care about our situation. Bridget, a freckled-faced girl, who always got on my nerves, said like a brat, "Everyone knows girls are best."

Then P. J. shouted, "We're not going to stand for this." P. J. was smart and well liked by the fifth grade teachers. "We're going on strike!" he screamed.

Then shouts of "strike" started to build within the boys. "Strike, strike, strike, strike," came rushing out.

I turned to Bobby and asked him what a strike was.

"I thought it was when you knock all the pins down while you are bowling," I said.

"It's also when you stop working, which means we won't go to the classrooms when school starts," said Bobby.

"I'm in," I said jubilantly.

Then someone added, "No show, no school; no show, no school; no show, no school."

The teachers did not take us seriously. I think the teachers were quite amused and impressed, especially when we started to make our protesting picket signs. We got the paper and markers from the art room.

Ring. That was the first bell. School was about to start. The strikers started disappearing.

"What's going on?" I said aloud.

Then the second bell rang, which was the tardy bell, or the you're-in–trouble-for-being-very-late bell. Just a handful of us remained. "School is starting and I'm on strike," I thought. The tardy bell had rung. What did it matter how late I was going to be.

Common sense took over and I decided to go back

to Mr. Phillips' class. When I walked in, I noticed there was a chalk circle up on the blackboard.

"Jimmy," he said, "you're late."

I knew the routine.

"Nice picket sign by the way," Mr. Phillips said sarcastically.

The teachers finally gave in and allowed some of the boys in the show. I think the teachers were impressed that we had organized our strike and that we really cared about the show. However, not all of the boys were allowed to perform, including myself. I was disappointed, but I knew I had a long way to go in order to play as Grandpa did.

Ike, who played a song under his armpits, was not allowed to compete either. I thought he was very impressive. The teachers thought he was gross. No one wanted to touch his stinky hands. The teachers made him wash his hands afterwards. Ike and I sat next to each other at the show.

Not a single boy got first place, second place, or third place. Natalie, a gymnast, got first; Jean, a singer, got second place. A second-grade girl named Isabelle who twirled baton got third. I think she got third because she dropped it.

"I'll be back," I vowed to myself.

The next school day, I brought my spoons to school and started to practice. The noise caught Mr. Phillips' attention.

"Jimmy," he yelled.

"Oh, boy, here we go again," I thought—up to the little circle on the blackboard.

"You're good at that," said Mr. Phillips with encouragement in his voice.

That was all I needed to hear. For some reason on that hot and humid late spring day, those words echoed in my mind. They gave me the confidence and motivation I needed to continue to practice. Even to this day, I remember those words, "Jimmy, you're good at that." They were just four simple words from a teacher to whom I looked up.

Chapter 8

# Johnny's Idea

After school, I raced home to my neighbor Johnny's house. He lived right across the street from us. I met Johnny in his dad's workshop, which was also their garage.

Frustrated, I said, "Whenever I try it, Johnny, the spoons keep slipping apart. Watch closely, I'll show you what my grandpa taught me."

Johnny could see that the spoons were slipping.

"Well, it sounded great for a while," Johnny said. "Wait a minute. I have a great idea on how we can keep them from slipping apart."

Johnny held up a small white-and-green pointed-tipped plastic bottle that he had gotten out of his dad's woodworking cabinet.

"What is it?" I asked curiously.

"It's some sort of special strength super glue," he said. "Hold out your hand and we'll put a little bit on the handles. Maybe that will help."

"Okay," I said with some hesitation.

Johnny squeezed with all of his might. Loads of

glue was spilling out on the spoons, on my hand, and on the garage floor.

"Whoa, slow down," I said.

The glue felt ice cold and smelled horrible at first, then the smell started to go away.

"Hold on tight to those spoons," Johnny instructed me.

I held the spoons tightly with all my might for about five minutes.

"Try it now," he commanded.

To my amazement, it really worked.

"I can do it," I shouted loudly. "Look at me now, Johnny, I'm almost as good as my grandpa." The spoons were not slipping apart as I played on my legs, arms, chest, and feet. "Look at me go," I yelled.

In fact, the spoons would not even come out of my hands.

"What's the matter? Why did you stop playing? You were doing great," asked Johnny curiously.

"I can't let go of the spoons," I said nervously.

The spoons would not budge from my hand. Then I

heard in the distance, “Jimmy, time for dinner!” It was my mother calling me home.

“What am I going to do?” I said to Johnny with panic in my voice.

Johnny just smirked and said, “I don’t know.”

“Jimmy,” my mother called again, “time to eat.”

“All right, Mom. I’ll be there in a minute,” I shouted back.

I was praying that it was soup or a sandwich or something that I could eat in one hand.

“Tell your mom that you’re practicing holding the spoons and maybe the glue will wear off eventually,” Johnny said.

“Eventually? Gee, thanks for your help,” I complained.

As I walked across the street, I stuck my right hand in my front jean pocket. When I approached the front yard, the smell hit me like a ton of bricks. It was my favorite dinner in the entire world. Mom had made barbecued spare ribs and corn on the cob.

"I made your favorite, Jimmy," she said as I walked through the front door.

"It's impossible to eat this delicious meal with one hand. What am I going to do?" I thought.

"I'm not hungry, Mom," I said, starving.

"What? You're not hungry?" she said surprised. "You said you were starving before you went over to Johnny's. I made this dinner just for you. You know your sisters don't really like to eat ribs. Sit down and get your hand out of your pocket and start eating!"

"What's in your pocket?" my sister Susie asked slyly.

"Nothing," I said abruptly.

Susie's little question was enough to set my mother's suspicions in motion. My mom leaned over and saw the spoons in my right hand.

"Jimmy, drop those spoons now and eat your dinner before it gets cold," she said angrily.

My sister Susie knew there was something wrong, so she repeated what my mother had said.

"Yea, Jimmy, let go of those spoons and start to eat," she said giggling.

"But Mom, I'm practicing holding the spoons the right way, the way that Grandpa taught me," I said quickly.

"You can practice after dinner," she said.

I knew I was sunk, and it was time to tell the truth.

"Mom, I can't let go of the spoons; they're glued to my hand. Johnny and I thought it would be a good idea to put a little glue on the spoons to hold them together. Some of the glue got on my hands and I can't let go," I said apologetically.

Mom's face turned as red as a tomato because of her anger. The last time I saw my mother this angry was years ago when she did not let me watch Frosty the Snowman on television. My sisters, seeing our tomato-faced mother and me with spoons stuck to my right hand, started to laugh aloud.

"This is no joking matter," my mother snapped back at my sisters.

My mother escorted me like a prisoner into the

bathroom. She reached into one of the cabinets and pulled out a small lavender-colored vase-shaped container.

"Put your right hand over the sink," she instructed.

She carefully opened the bottle and poured the contents over my right hand.

"Yuck," I screamed. "What's that smell?"

My hand started to feel cold as if she was pouring ice water over it. My mother reached for the switch on the wall to turn the vent on and opened the bathroom window.

"What you smell is nail polish remover, and it can be dangerous if inhaled. That's why I opened the window and turned on the fan," she said. "Now see if you can get the spoons out of your hand."

The spoons dropped to the bottom of the sink. Clink Clank. It sounded like handcuffs falling to the floor. I started to wash that horrific smell from my hands.

"How did you know that the nail polish remover would also remove the glue?" I asked my mother.

"Mothers know these things," she said. "Now get back to the dinner table and start eating."

Chapter 9

# Going to Work

The next day, I could not wait to get home from school to practice. I was determined to play just like Grandpa. I pulled out my old creaky wooden chair and sat down. I turned on my transistor radio to find some music. Again, I had trouble playing. Maybe I was just missing some of Grandpa's coaching. After many hours of trying, it still would not work. Then I remembered when I first rode my bicycle and how I kept falling down and wanted to quit.

"I can't do it, Dad. I'm tired of trying. I'll never learn how to ride this bike," I said discouraged.

"You need to have patience, Jimmy, he said. "Look at these tulips in our garden. Do you see how the buds haven't bloomed yet? What would happen if I tried to make them bloom by opening them with my fingers?"

"You would probably wreck the whole tulip," I said.

"Jimmy, we have to wait for them to bloom on their own. We need to be patient just like the tulips."

My father kept on encouraging me.

"If you can do this, you can do anything," he said.

After practicing every day for a week, I was finally

able to ride my bicycle. “That’s right,” I thought. “I can do anything.”

On the thirty-third try, I had the basic spoon grip down. I knew I had a lot more to learn in order to play like Grandpa, but at least I had the grip down.

I finally had my musical outlet—my imaginary drum set in the palm of my hand. From that point on, I carried my spoons with me wherever I went. I ate with my spoons next to me, slept with my spoons in my hands, did my homework with my spoons, took a shower with my spoons, and went to school with my spoons in my back pocket. People started to call me “Spoonboy.” My spoons went wherever I went. I loved my spoons.

After playing the spoons for a while, I noticed it was easier putting my thumb off to the side of the spoons, to make a space, rather than using my pointer finger. I also discovered that wrapping athletic tape around each handle made the spoons easier to hold. They did not slip around in my hand as much.

“I can’t wait to show my classmates how much I’ve

improved," I said to myself.

The next day I decided to wear long pants to school rather than shorts to cover up the bruises on my legs. My legs were not as swollen as they were when I first started practicing. I discovered that you did not have to hit yourself hard to make a sound with the spoons. All you had to do was just a little tap. My grandpa never had bruises on his legs because all you had to do was tap lightly.

Politely I asked, "Mr. Phillips, can I show you something that I've been working on?"

It was toward the end of the school year, and I knew Mr. Phillips was a little more understanding about what we could get away with.

"Sure," he said.

I pulled out my spoons and started to play.

"Jimmy, that sounds great," Mr. Phillips exclaimed. "I can tell that you've been practicing."

"Wow, that sounds great," shouted several class members.

"Now it's time to put those spoons away and to get

to work," said Mr. Phillips.

"Well, at least he was somewhat understanding," I said to myself.

I finally discovered something at which I was good. Not just anyone could do my special talent. I could not wait to get home from school to practice. Unfortunately, this evening was grocery-shopping night.

"Mom, is it all right if I bring my spoons?" I asked.

"Sure, Jimmy, as long as you keep them in your pocket. You don't want anyone to think that you stole them," she said.

At least, I could bring my spoons with me while we shop. "Who knows," I thought. "Maybe my spoons will come in handy for some candy, candy, candy."

Chapter 10

# The Candy

My sister Susie and I were like two hungry vultures that had not eaten in weeks, ready to pounce on the boy's mistake. I would have rather stayed home to practice my spoons, but the possibility of getting candy, candy, candy was exciting.

Friday night was grocery night at Meijer, my mother's favorite store. The routine was for my mother to drop Susie and me off in the toy section while she went shopping with Lori. My sister Lori was not too happy with this arrangement. I thought Lori was lucky; she received all kinds of snacks while being pushed through the store. My mother would always pick us up at a designated time and location. The location was by checkout lane number five. For Susie and me, our mission was candy. We did not care how we got it. We just knew we had to have it.

"Candy, candy, candy, give us lots of candy." We were singing and skipping down the toy aisle.

Our destination was the gumball machines. The machines were located just inside the entrance of the store. They were stacked one on top of another. It was a multi-colored pyramid of gumballs, Sweet Tarts, and assorted hard candies.

We knew it would be a matter of time before a mistake was made. When we arrived, we scanned the area for children. There was none. We scanned the floor for loose change. There was none. We stuck our pointer fingers carefully in each little metal swinging door. Sometimes kids would leave some candy behind, especially if it came out in a handful.

"Nothing," Susie said disappointedly.

To my pleasant surprise, I heard a voice off in the distance.

"I want candy, Mommy. Now. Please, please, please," he said.

He had red curly hair with freckles, and he was somewhat plump—no doubt from all the candy he had feasted on in his five short years of life.

"I want that one—the giant, orange, super-duper bubble-blowing gumball," he said.

"Okay, Billy," his mother said in a frustrated manner.

I could tell the mother was irritated. She was struggling to hold a one-year-old baby girl who wanted to get down and join in on the fun. It was the ideal setup—an angry mother and a whining child.

She hurriedly looked through her enormous purse. First her hand disappeared and then her entire elbow. I had never seen a purse so large in all my ten years. There were so many items in her purse; it was as loud as digging through a bag of metal tools.

“Hurry up, Mommy,” sugar-craving Billy insisted. “I want the dime now.”

I saw the mother’s right arm emerge from her purse with a bright shiny new dime. She held it up high in her fingertips. She was proudly displaying what she had found in her enormous purse. Like a frog snatching a fly in midair, Billy pounced on the new coin.

“Thanks, Mommy,” he said quickly.

Well, at least he was polite. Billy went right for the colossal orange gumball that looked like a painted golf ball. Billy, with his dime pinched between his plump little fingers, inserted the money.

Susie and I knew that with that gumball machine, nine out of ten times, the gumball would go flying through the swinging metal door and bounce onto the floor. The only way to stop it was to hold your hand very tight next to the shiny swinging door so it would not fly out.

The mother now noticed Susie and I lurking. She gave us both an uneasy glare like a deer in headlights. Billy slowly turned the handle clockwise. My heart was thumping like a drum in anticipation of what was going to happen. Susie was clinching my forearm tightly.

Clink, clink, clunk. Billy quickly reached towards the metal garage door. He opened the door and out jumped the orange golf-ball-sized gumball right onto the floor.

"No, no, no," Billy started to cry out. "I want that one. I don't care if it has a million germs."

"Absolutely not," shouted his mother.

"I want that one. I don't want another one," screamed Billy uncontrollably. People were starting to stare at the scene Billy was making.

I felt bad for the mother because of the way Billy was acting. What could I do? My spoons, maybe I could play for Billy. I had never played in front of strangers before. I guess now would be a good time. I reached into my back pocket, pulled out my spoons, and started to play. Immediately Billy stopped crying and walked over near me. His mother was looking on very suspiciously.

"What's that?" he said curiously.

"Hold out your hands and I'll show you," I said.

I started to play the spoons on the palm of Billy's hand.

"Wow! Look at this, Mommy. That's cool," he said excitedly. "I've been spooned, Mommy."

"Yes," I thought, "you've been spooned by Spoonboy."

With the break in the crying action, his mother was able to find another dime in her purse and hand it over to Billy.

"You're right, that's neat," said Billy's mother. "Here's another dime for you and two more dimes for your new friends."

"Thank you so much," I said.

"Yeah, thanks," said Susie.

"Billy, this time, my sister and I will help you so the gumball doesn't go flying," I said.

I put my spoons back into my pocket and whispered to them, "Good job."

We all had a gumball now and everyone was happy.

Normally, Susie and I would watch the screaming child be pulled away, and then we would pick up the gumball and take it to the bathroom. We would run very hot water over it to kill the germs. Then Susie and I would break the gumball in half and chow down. Helping Billy was much more rewarding.

Susie and I went to our meeting point at checkout number five. We spotted Lori sitting in the grocery cart covered with chocolate.

"Where did you get gum?" my mother asked both of us.

"Jimmy played his spoons for a little boy who was crying. His mother bought us both a gumball," Susie said.

"Wow, that was kind of her," said our mother.

"Maybe Jimmy could give our ears a break and play spoons over at that little boy's house," my mother said teasing me.

"Real funny, Mom," I said.

"We need to hurry home to get the groceries unpacked. Your father and I are working on a little surprise for you," she said again with a teasing smile.

"Surprise?" we said together. "Tell us now, tell us now!"

"We'll tell you when school gets out for the summer. You only have a few more days to wait," she said.

## Chapter 11

# The Move

It was summer and the surprise was about to be revealed.

"Jimmy, Susie, and Lori, sit down on the couch. Your mother and I have something we want to tell you," said my Dad.

"Wow, this must be important. Very rarely are we called to sit on the couch all together. Maybe we're going to get a huge swimming pool this summer or a dog," I thought.

My dad had straight jet-black hair with hazel eyes. He was stricter and more serious than my mother was. As we sat down on the rust-colored sofa, our jaws dropped to the ground as my father announced we would be moving.

"We're going to build a new house in a new city," Dad said excitedly.

"Why can't we build a new house around here?" I asked.

I had many friends in our neighborhood, many more than my sisters did. It was almost an all-boy neighborhood. We played football, hockey, basketball, and baseball. We had sleepovers in each other's homes and in tents. We rode our bikes together everywhere. Now we were going to leave.

"Hooray! Hooray!" shouted my sister Susie.

"Shut up," I said angrily.

Yelling at my sister got me quickly directed into my bedroom.

"Hooray! Hooray!" continued my sister Susie.

I could hear her yelling all the way from my bedroom. "That's enough now," my dad said, noticing that Susie was excited but she also was trying to tease me.

I could still hear my mom and dad talking.

"We're going to build a two-story house. Susie and Lori, you'll both have your own bedrooms," said my mother.

"Hooray!" said my sister Lori just once.

"We're going to have a bigger house with a swimming pool, and we'll be near Buck Creek which has brown trout," said my dad.

He added the creek part because he knew I was

listening from my bedroom.

“Can we go to the same school?” I shouted from my bedroom.

“You‘ll be going to a new school called South Elementary,” said my mother.

“Hooray! Hooray!” shouted my sister Susie who did not have many friends at school.

“Hooray!” yelled my sister Lori.

I do not know why Lori shouted hooray when she had not even started school yet.

“Oh no,” I said sadly.

I was popular and considered cool at our school. I was starting to become known as Spoonboy. I was not happy about changing schools.

“Can I take a bus back to my old school?” I shouted down the hallway.

“No. That’s out of the question. We’re going to be too far away,” Dad said.

I knew I had to make this summer in my neighborhood the best ever. One good thing about summer was that my sister Susie and I did not have to go to bed earlier than Lori did. There was no need to spy during the summertime.

After all the news from my parents settled in, I reached into my back pocket and pulled out my pair of spoons. I sat in my old brown wooden chair and turned on my Panasonic radio. I closed my eyes, pretending I was on stage at a concert wailing away on my spoons. Practicing the spoons helped me not to worry about the future and leaving the best neighborhood ever.

During the summer, I wanted to teach as many kids as I could how to play spoons, so they would not forget me. This caused a problem at home. You see, I used our spoons instead of theirs.

Chapter 12

# Missing Spoons

During the summer months, my mother's spoons started to disappear. Some I left outside in the backyard, others at my friends' houses, under the couch, or down in the basement. However, I always knew the location of my favorite pair. I never used them for eating or for showing others how to play.

One summer morning, my dad got angry with me.

"There's not one single spoon in this silverware drawer," he shouted loudly at me.

My dad had a huge bowl of expensive five fruit cereal. This cereal was so special that you could not even buy it at a normal grocery store. The more seconds that ticked by, the soggier the expensive cereal became, and the angrier my father grew.

He opened the dishwasher to find two dirty spoons with caked mashed potatoes from last night's dinner. When you leave mashed potatoes overnight on a spoon, it hardens like cement. My dad's face was turning red as his blood pressure started to boil. My mom was not home this morning, so I had to face his anger head on.

It was my fault there were no spoons. My irresponsibility finally caught up with me. I thought for a moment that maybe I should let him use one of my playing spoons that I had in my back pocket. Thinking again, I became certain that I was not going to volunteer my spoons unless he demanded them from me.

By now, the expensive cereal looked like a bowl of mushy paste. It had a red tint to it from the dried strawberries, one of the five fruits.

"Jimmy, come over here," my dad demanded.

I hesitantly moved toward him, wondering what he was going to tell me.

Looking down at the sick, soggy, mushy, slimy bowl of cereal, my dad stared at me squarely in the eyes and said, "Eat it, now."

"I'm not hungry," I said nervously.

"This is your breakfast. You will eat it now and in front of me."

"Can't I have peanut butter toast like Susie and Lori did?"

"No," he said again.

I was starting to think that I wanted no part of the lesson he was trying to teach me.

"Dad, why don't you have some toast for breakfast instead of cereal? We have some great whole wheat bread that Mom bought along with fresh strawberry jam," I said.

This question made my father even angrier.

"Close your mouth and eat your cereal now," he stated.

Again, the thought crossed my mind to use one of my own spoons. My dad was so angry I could not take the risk that he would not grab them right out of my hand and I would never see them again. It was still going to taste the same whether it was in my spoons or in my hand. I reached my right hand into the pinkish milky slime, which was now warm. I cradled the slimy mush into the palm of my right hand and started to slurp it up. I started to gag as it slipped down my throat. I swallowed hard. My dad, thank God, did not make me finish the whole bowl.

"That's enough, Jimmy. I want you to remember what it's like not having any spoons to eat with," he said smiling.

He was smiling because he knew that I had learned a lesson.

"You can start looking for our missing spoons that you've scattered all over our house and around the neighborhood," he said.

That summer morning, I found six sets of spoons. From that day forward, I made sure that there were always spoons in the silverware drawer, especially during my father's breakfast.

It was getting toward the end of summer and we were preparing to move. Every time I thought about going to a new school, butterflies started to explode deep within my stomach.

My mother thought it would be a good idea if we took a little break from packing.

"Tomorrow, we're going horseback riding," she said.

"Cool," I shouted enthusiastically.

"Not cool," my sister Susie said stubbornly. What a strange response! Neither of us had ever been horseback riding before.

"Oh, Susie, this is going to be an adventure. You're going to love this," our mother said.

Boy, was it ever an adventure!

Chapter 13

# Runaway Horse

It was a hot humid Tuesday afternoon in the late summer. I was not sure if I should bring my spoons with me horseback riding or not. Maybe they would come in handy like they had for Billy at the grocery store. I decided to bring them.

When we arrived at the Smitty's Resort and Ranch, a tall, thin, wiry-looking teenager named Joe greeted us. He wore a dirty white T-shirt with a bright yellow nametag clipped to his waist. He had long stringy hair, and it looked like he was trying to grow a beard on the tip of his chin. I could tell he was tired and had no interest working with us. It was just a summer job to him, and teenagers have other things on their minds.

"This is Blazer, and this is Lightning," he said with no emotion.

My mother watched what was going on from a distance. She had no plans to ride with my little sister Lori.

Lightning was black and white. He almost looked like a zebra. Blazer was milk chocolate brown and younger than my horse, which meant it had less experience with people.

"Remember, a horse can tell if you're afraid and it can also tell if you know how to control it. You need to show your horse who's the boss by holding the reins tight. You might even have to give him a little kick in the side," said Joe in an uninterested manner. It sounded as if he was reading from a script.

As soon as we were both saddled up, I could tell there was something wrong with Blazer and my sister. Blazer knew that my sister was afraid and would not know how to control him. Blazer took advantage of my sister's timid approach and slowly walked over to some weeds and started to eat before we even got to the trail. This was not a good sign. Lightning saw this and started to move toward Blazer. I quickly grabbed the reins and pulled back. Lightning got the idea quickly. Blazer kept on eating. Joe was not concerned with what was going on.

"Let's go," Joe shouted to the whole group, which consisted of seven riders.

Blazer listened reluctantly and walked slowly behind Joe's horse and the rest of us followed. Joe was leading us on the dusty winding trail that went through fields and deep dark woods. I could tell right away that I should not have worn my favorite Levi shorts. Every time we went into the woods, swarms of mosquitoes attacked us like a squadron of B-52 bombers.

Before we started on our ride, I asked Joe, "Should we be concerned about the mosquitoes?"

"No, don't worry about it. They aren't bad at all," he said with little care.

In no time at all, my legs were speckled with tiny red bumps from the vampire-like bloodsucking bugs. I wished I had on my long pants or at least had some bug spray. Everyone else, including my sister Susie, and except Joe, had worn long pants. He had shorts on like me, but the mosquitoes were not attacking him. I think he had sprayed his legs with mosquito repellent that he was not going to share.

"Gee, Joe. It's funny the mosquitoes aren't attacking

you," I said.

"Gee, you're right," he said with a mocking voice. Joe laughed when he glanced toward my swollen red-dotted legs.

Once we came out of the woods, I thought, "Great, no more mosquitoes." Then Joe said, "Let's try this new trail over here."

From a distance, the trail looked inviting. It wound through a golden field of wheat. You could tell when the wind blew across the field; the wheat would roll back and forth like a wavy ocean. What I did not see were the berry bushes with thorns that were as sharp as tiny little knives. Again, no one else was bothered—just me in my shorts. Joe was sitting up high enough on his horse so the brush was not touching his legs. My legs looked like a tic-tac-toe game. Along with all the red bumps, I had crisscrossed lines all over.

"This is worse than the woods," I moaned. "Please, can we go to that creek bed?"

"Whatever," Joe said, uninterested.

This is where the real problem started. Every horse crossed into the creek bed except Blazer. He made it halfway through the creek and just stopped. Blazer had decided not to go any further, and Susie could not do anything about it. He shifted his head and looked at the other horses. The other horses continued to move further and further away down the trail. Blazer, as well as my sister, panicked. Blazer bolted in the opposite direction down the creek bed and into the woods as if someone had just branded him with a hot glowing metal rod. My sister Susie's legs were waving up and down as she bounced on top of her brown leather saddle. She looked like an octopus trying to ride a horse. I could hear my sister's screams echoing through the forest.

"Help, help, somebody help me!" said Susie fearing for her life.

Blazer dashed into the tiny creek bed towards the deep black forest carrying my screaming, arm-swinging sister.

"Grab the reins!" Joe screamed.

"Grab the reins and hold tight," I shouted also.

Our screams and shouts did not help. I could see the reins flopping in the air. My sister was bouncing up and down holding on to the saddle with all her might. Joe was panic-stricken. I could tell he did not know what to do.

"This has never happened before," he kept repeating to himself.

We could not hear Susie's voice anymore; it just melted into the dark mosquito-infested forest. All of a sudden, Blazer, to my sister's relief, decided to stop. Perhaps Blazer realized he was not at the Kentucky Derby. Susie, full of tears, quickly jumped off and began to run as if she was in the Kentucky Derby. Where she was running, she did not know. She just wanted to get away from Blazer as fast as possible. Susie ran and ran as fast as she could and ended up in the middle of a nearby cornfield.

"I'll never ever ride a horse again!" she screamed.

She continued to run through the cornfield until she was swallowed up in a sea of corn. There was another little problem. It was late summer, and the corn was about seven feet tall; Susie was about four feet tall. She did not know which way to go. Everything looked the same. All she could see were rows of corn in every direction.

"Well, at least Blazer won't be able to find me. But then again, maybe no one else will either," she sobbed.

Blazer showed up at the ranch a few minutes later, trotting along as happy as could be— rider-less, of course. This really panicked Joe. Was Susie injured? Was she safe? Could she walk? Joe nervously called into home base with his walkie–talkie. His hands were shaking as if he had just downed a two-liter bottle of Mountain Dew.

The head of the horse ranch Cowboy Craig yelled at him severely for his irresponsibility. I actually felt sorry for Joe. Cowboy Craig organized three search parties.

"Can I come? I'm her brother!" I asked full of excitement.

I was not too afraid that my sister was missing. I just wanted to help find her.

"Sure," said Craig, "we need some strong voices."

I lifted my spoons straight up in the air as if they were swords. I was a soldier riding on horseback to come to the aid of the lost damsel in distress. No one had told my mom what was going on.

The sun was starting to sink lower in the sky and Susie was getting hungry. Susie decided to sit and wait for someone to find her.

Clip clop, clip clop, the horses were walking over some pavement in search of Susie. Hey, I realized I could make that same rhythm with my spoons. I pulled out my spoons from my back pocket. I noticed that they were warmer than normal, probably from Lightning's body heat.

"Susie! Susie!" shouts were launched into the humid summer air. I was amazed that my mother could not hear anything. Maybe she could not hear because she was sitting in the car trying to occupy my sister Lori.

Clip clop, clip clop. I made my spoons mimic the trot.

"I sound just like the horses," I said.

The rhythms of the spoons were echoing all over the woods and fields.

"Wow," I said. "This really echoes out here."

I was tapping the spoons off Lightning's back. Lightning had been spooned, and he seemed to like it. This was fun. It was as if I was having a concert for Mother Nature.

In between the shouts for Susie, Craig said, "That's pretty good. Keep playing. Maybe she'll be able to hear you."

"Oh, no. Blazer is coming back after me again," Susie thought as she heard my spooning rhythms.

"Wait a minute. That sounds like my brother's spoons," she said.

"I'm here; I'm over here," Susie shouted with joy.

Craig could hear her in the cornfield but could not see her.

"Keep playing the spoons and I'll come to you," yelled Susie.

"Jimmy, keep those spoons going. Susie is going to follow the beats right out of the cornfield," said Craig.

"I'm like the Pied Piper," I thought.

"There she is," shouted Craig. "Keep playing those

spoons, Spoonboy. She's almost here."

Susie ran out of the cornfield right into the arms of Craig. I could see a sigh of relief in everyone's face, especially the face of Joe. We went back to our car where my mother was wiping chocolate off my sister Lori's face.

"How was your ride?" my mother asked excitedly.

"It was an adventure," I said.

"Never again, never again," snarled Susie like an ornery lion.

Susie was too tired to talk about it anymore.

"Mom, Susie got lost and I came to the rescue. I was a soldier riding my horse with my spoons glimmering in the sun," I shouted.

"Don't you mean swords," she said.

"No, my spoons. My spoons saved Susie," I said proudly.

"We'll talk more about it when we get home," she said.

I was sure glad I had brought my spoons. Who would have thought that my spoons were going to help during our rescue mission? I wondered if my spoons would be able to help me when I went to my new school.

Moving was a week away. I was sad about leaving the best neighborhood ever, and I was afraid and nervous about going to a new school. What would the school be like? Would my teacher be nice? Would the kids be kind? Whom would I sit next to during lunch? Whom would I play with at recess? I tossed and turned all night long pondering these questions.

## Chapter 14

# The New School

"Please state your name," said Mrs. Scrips. She was my fifth grade teacher at my new school, South Elementary. Mrs. Scrips was very different from Mr. Phillips. She was older than Mr. Phillips was, and she had some gray hair. She wore round black little glasses that balanced on the tip of her nose. The weirdest thing about her classroom was that we had no desks. We had to sit at multi-colored round tables with other students, and we had to keep our supplies in the colored plastic rectangular tubs. I thought it was very strange to have tubs rather than our own desks.

"Please state your name," she said again to someone else.

"My name is Joellyn," said a brown-haired girl sitting at my table.

"Joellyn," I said to myself. "What a strange name." I rather giggled. Joellyn quickly glared at me with displeasure.

"Please state your name," Mrs. Scrips said again.

"My name is Russell," said this kid with pin straight

hair and funny looking black glasses.

"What a geek with those glasses," I thought.

My heart was beating like a runaway freight train because I knew it was my turn next. How should I behave, should I be funny, should I be shy, should I play my spoons, or should I just be quiet? I decided that I should be funny. People liked me at my old school because I was so funny.

"Please state your name," she said.

"Jimmy unga bunga unga bunga bunga," I said proudly.

This line always got a laugh at my old school. However, my new fellow classmates just stared in disbelief. Amy, a tall blonde girl, pointed out that I had spoons in my back pocket. Joellyn covered her mouth trying not to spill her laughter all over our table. She was not laughing at what I said, she was laughing at how foolish I looked. Russell kind of chuckled and then rolled his eyes. Mrs. Scrips just ignored the "unga bunga" part along with why I had spoons in my pocket and carried on with her class introductions. "Well," I thought to myself, "at least she doesn't do the chalkboard punishment."

When it was time for lunch in the cafeteria, people started pairing up in small groups to sit and eat. Where was I going to sit? Everyone thought I was a weirdo. A few kids were new to the school just like me. Russell was one of those new kids. He had a spot open, so I decided to sit down next to him and eat my lunch.

"Where're you from?" asked Russell. "Why do you carry spoons in your pocket?"

"I moved here from Kentwood, and I carry spoons because I like to play them as a musical instrument like you would a drum set," I said.

"What do you mean by a musical instrument?" he asked.

"Let me show you," I replied.

I pulled out my spoons and started tapping gently on my leg. People started to turn around in the cafeteria, wondering what was going on.

"Wow, that's really cool," said Russell.

"That's great, Jimmy," shouted some other people

who were gathering around.

"Look at Spoonboy playing his spoons," screamed Joellyn.

Daniel, the only redheaded boy in the entire school, was in charge of the record player and all the music at lunch. He pulled out a Beach Boys album from the closet and started to play it. I was now spooning to the rhythm of the music.

"Let me try," Russell asked.

At first, he could not do it. After showing him how to hold the spoons, Russell was almost as good as I was.

"That's awesome," he said.

Other people tried, but they could not do it as well as Russell and I could. Russell became one of my good friends, especially after I had to get glasses. The glasses I picked out were just like his!

As the weeks and months passed by, I noticed a big difference in my grades. For the first time in my life, I was getting As, instead of Cs and Ds. I was concentrating more on my schoolwork rather then getting into trouble and trying to make people laugh.

My spoon playing became old news after a while. People were actually getting annoyed with my playing. Daniel would not even play records anymore during lunch. Then something horrible happened. My favorite spoons in the entire world were kidnapped, or should I say, they were spoon-napped!

Chapter 15

# The Kidnapped Spoons

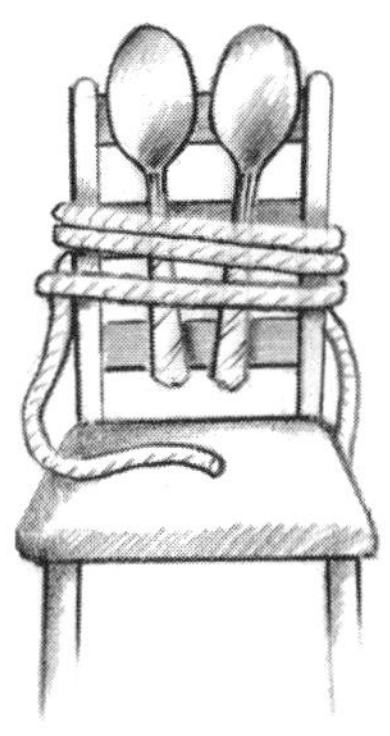

On a blue-skied Friday afternoon towards the end of the day, I went to get my books out of my colored school tub.

"Where are they?" I shouted loudly. My heart was racing like a horse. "My spoons!" I shouted loudly again. "Where are they?"

My classmates just stared at me as they normally did, not saying anything. Maybe I heard one little chuckle.

"Oh the pain, oh the horror," I thought. Those spoons were like part of my body. They were like fingers on my hand.

My favorite spoons went everywhere with me except recess. During recess, I did not want them falling out of my pocket so I kept them in my stupid, stinky, colored little tub—the tub that everyone could get into without any trouble.

"Russell, you've got to help me. Where are they? Who took them? Did you see anything strange going on? Please, please help me?" I pleaded.

"I don't know," Russell said calmly. "I'll do what I

can to help. Why don't you ask Daniel?"

Daniel never liked my spoon playing and he never liked me. I quickly went over to Daniel.

"Okay, Daniel, where are my spoons?"

"I don't know," he said with a funny looking face. "Maybe YOU lost them, maybe YOU didn't put them back in your tub, maybe it's all YOUR fault," Daniel said with anger.

Mrs. Scrips seemed unconcerned about our voices being raised. Maybe it was because the school day had just about ended.

"I know where I put them," I screamed back at Daniel. "Someone kidnapped them out of my tub."

Daniel just shrugged his shoulders and walked away.

After school, I was so upset; I decided to walk home instead of taking the bus. I had a strong feeling that I was being followed. I turned my head slowly to the right and noticed out of the corner of my eye an older kid, possibly a sixth grader. Whatever street I turned down, he followed me cautiously. I finally decided to put an end to his little game and approached him. He had a green army jacket, long brown hair, and he smelled like old French fries. The tiny long black hairs on his chin were all curled up forming a perfect circle.

"Do you want something?" I said in an aggravated manner. I was not in a very good mood.

"The question is do you want something?" he said. "My name is Rich. I might know where your spoons are."

I gasped. "You do? Give them to me now," I demanded.

I had to be careful how I talked to Rich. He was a whole head taller than I was.

"You'll be given instructions on Monday. If you ever want to see your spoons alive again, you'll listen to my warning," he said secretively.

Rich added the word "alive" to make it sound more dramatic. It was dramatic enough already.

"Okay," I said angrily. "I guess I have no choice."

Rich slowly slipped away, down through the twisting

snakelike streets.

That weekend was the longest weekend in my entire life. What were the demands going to be? Would it be money? I did not have a job. “Maybe I could sell one of my sisters,” I thought. I would do anything to get my spoons back.

Just then, I heard a boom, boom, thud, thud. My mother had just started her evening cleaning ritual. Because we were in a two-story house, my mother could not hear Susie and me doing our evening talk.

“What time is it?” Susie said.

“I don’t know and I don’t care,” I said sadly.

The only thing I could think of was getting to school on Monday and finding my precious spoons.

“Goodnight, my friends, wherever you are,” I whispered softly into the air.

“What day is it?” Susie asked.

I think she was trying to cheer me up. I just ignored her, closed my eyes, and dreamed about Monday morning.

Chapter 16

# The Dumpster

I tossed and turned all night until Monday morning finally came. When I got to school, I quickly jumped off the bus scanning the playground, eagerly looking for Rich. He was nowhere to be found. I was feeling a lot of anxiety because the first bell was about to ring. Just then, a strange odor caught my attention. "French fries," I thought. It was Rich. He found me.

"If you give me your Twinkies for the next month, I'll tell you where your spoons are," he said. "Now keep in mind it wasn't me who took your spoons. I just happen to know where they are."

"Who took them?" I demanded to know.

"I didn't see anyone take them. I just know where they are," Rich said calmly. "Do we have a deal?"

"Yes," I said, full of panic. "Where are they?" I cried louder.

Just then, the first bell rang. When the first bell rang, it meant that we had five minutes to make it to our classroom. Rich could tell that I was getting very nervous.

"Relax," he said. "Your spoons are wrapped up in

some old tin foil from someone's lunch."

"Okay, okay. Where do I look?" I pleaded. "Four minutes till the final bell rings," I thought.

"They're in the huge green garbage dumpster in the back of the school," Rich said very slowly.

"That'll be like looking for a needle in a haystack," I thought.

Ring, ring, ring. That was the final bell. Rich and I were both going to be tardy.

Looking straight into my eyes, he said slowly and deliberately, "I'm not worried about being late. Remember to bring my Twinkies tomorrow."

I had never been tardy at my new school. I was also a straight A student. "Too late anyway," I said to myself. I have to complete my mission. My spoons had to be rescued.

The playground was empty. Everyone was in class. As I approached the monster dumpster, I could see what looked like a thousand bees. Not only could I see them, I could also hear their eerie buzzing sound. These bees were desperately trying to get into the dumpster.

I could smell sour milk all around the dumpster.

There was white milk, brown milk, and pink milk splattered all over the ground. It looked like someone had created a complicated painting.

As I flipped over the lid, the bees dove right into the dumpster, totally ignoring me. They were interested in the sweetness of the garbage. It was packed full of smelly rotted trash. It smelled like one of my sister Lori's dirty diapers.

I heard some rumbling like a huge truck coming from the distance. It was a garbage truck heading towards the school. My heart started beating out of control. I had not gone this far to stop now. I climbed up on the edge of the dumpster and plugged my nose. I hesitantly jumped feet first into the sea of sour milk, Twinkie wrappers, and buzzing bees. Squish, splash, slosh, splosh went my feet as I waded through the garbage.

I noticed half-finished peanut butter and jelly sandwiches turning a dark brown color and milk cartons that were half-full. The bees liked the spilled chocolate milk best. My favorite white Levi T-shirt and Levi jeans looked like they were tie-dyed now. As I was digging frantically for my spoons, I heard a beep, beep, beep. The garbage truck was getting into position to empty the trash container—with me inside!

Chapter 17

# The Dig

"No, no, no," I shouted in frustration. "I need more time! I need more time!"

The old grumbling diesel engine was so loud no one could hear me. Clink, clank! Two long curved octopus arms hooked into the top of the dumpster. The whole trash container started to shake. I could feel it being lifted off the ground.

"Stop," I screamed repeatedly. "Help, help!"

The garbage truck lifted the dumpster as high as it could, swinging the garbage and me backwards into the truck's waste compartment.

Clink, clank! I heard something that sounded like spoons as I was being somersaulted into the mountain of waste. It was wrapped in tin foil and it fell right at my feet.

"My spoons, my spoons!" I yelled with glee.

I quickly grabbed the foil and unwrapped an old toothbrush.

"Toothbrush?" I said disappointedly. It was covered with paint. Evidently, the art teacher used it for painting and threw it out.

My heart sank a million miles. "I'm never going to find my spoons," I thought.

Then I heard my grandpa in my thoughts, "Don't give up, Soldier. Pull yourself up and take a stand. You can do this." In the corner of my left eye, I noticed another piece of foil up near my head. I flung my right hand toward it and held tightly. From the moment my hand grabbed it, I knew what was inside. I quickly removed the foil and kissed both of my SPOONS.

Beep, beep, beep! I thought the truck was going to leave now, but it was not moving in any direction. To my horror, a big metal wall was starting to move slowly toward me. It was the trash compactor. I was going to die.

Mrs. Scrips was very concerned that I had not shown up for class. She started to question my classmates as to my whereabouts.

"Has anyone seen Jimmy this morning?" she asked.

"I saw him running towards the big dumpster as the bells were ringing. He was talking about finding his spoons," said Russell.

The walls were collapsing in on me slowly and deliberately. I had to think quickly. I could see and hear the compactor's metal gears turning. I had to stick something in the gears to jam it. All I could see were paper products. "My spoons, my spoons," I thought. "They are my swords of victory." I pulled out my precious spoons. "My poor precious spoons! What if they break? What if I break? What if I am crushed to death?" I said to myself. In the end, it was an easy choice. I quickly jammed both spoons into the oily black metal gears. I was afraid that one spoon would not be strong enough to stop the gears, so I used both. Creak, creak, clank, sputter, sputter.

"It worked! It worked!" I shouted joyously.

Beep, beep, beep! The compactor started to reverse directions.

Clank. My spoons fell to the bottom of the truck container.

"My beloved spoons saved my life!" I shouted triumphantly.

There was not even a dent in the spoons. I quickly

kissed them again and shoved them deeply into my pocket. I jumped out of the truck and sprang to the ground.

"I did it! I did it! I did it!"

Just as I finished my joyous shouts, I heard, "You sure did it all right. Your spoons won't save you from big trouble this time," said an angry, bewildered Mrs. Scrips.

Alongside her was Mr. Bradford, our principal. His eyebrows pointed straight up in the air and his mouth was frowning from cheek to cheek, and then there was his big purple-veined face, which I figured was caused by anger. For a moment, I thought I should jump back into the trash truck and ride away happily ever after with my spoons.

I was immediately sent home to shower and to change my clothes, which was fine with me. At least, I had my spoons. I was suspended from recess for a whole month, and my parents grounded me for the same amount of time. From that day forward, I never kept my spoons in my school tub again. They always stayed hidden, tucked away deep in my back pocket.

Chapter 18

# Lessons in Life

Not long after the spoon napping, my grandpa and I sat under the Buck Creek Bridge with our fly rods in hand trying to catch an elusive brown trout. With my spoon teacher next to me, I started to recall the changes, which had taken place in less than six months.

"Just think, Grandpa, we wouldn't be here right now if we hadn't moved."

My grandpa had just caught a 16-inch brown trout. It had bright red spots as large as nickels on its side, and it was golden brown. I had never caught one that big before. He soon caught another trout that was 17 inches long.

"You're right, Jimmy. I'm sure glad you moved here. The fishing is fantastic," he said.

I was starting to get discouraged because I had caught nothing.

"It looks to me like you're starting to get impatient. Remember, good things take time. Look at your spoon-playing skills. You're becoming very good because of your hard work. Who would have thought that you would've taken first place at your new school's talent show this spring?" he said.

"Look at the water we drink at our house. I could easily get water from the kitchen sink faucet to drink. However, the sweetest water is found outside at the bottom of our deep well. Sure, you have to pump and pump to get it out. It's the sweetest tasting water you could ever find. I could hook a trout for you, but it wouldn't be the same as if you hooked it yourself and caught it alone," he said.

Listening to the babbling water flowing over the multi-colored rocks along with my grandfather's flowing stories started to remind me of how things had really become different, not only on the outside but also on the inside.

"Jimmy, we're all like big walking treasure chests. Some of us discover our treasures right away. For others, it might take a bit of time. We should all help each other to discover our treasures," said Grandpa.

"I wish a brown trout would discover my fly right now," I said.

"Give it time, Jimmy," he said.

"It amazes me, Grandpa, that playing spoons can

affect people in so many ways," I said. "What would've happened to that little boy who was crying his head off if I hadn't had my spoons to calm him down? What would've happened to my sister when she was lost in the tall cornfield without my spoons making enough noises? What would've happened if I didn't have my spoons when the dumpster was going to crush me? What would've happened to me if I never found my little treasure of playing the spoons? I'll tell you what would've happened, Grandpa. I would've found another little treasure buried within me and I would make it shine just like my spoons."

At that moment, a big brown trout hit my fly, and I reeled him in.